I'VE ALWAYS HATED BEING STUCK IN THIS BACKWATER PART OF THE UNIVERSE.

WHEN YOU'RE STUCK IN THE MIDDLE OF NOWHERE, YOUR CAREER OPTIONS ARE FEW.

YOU'RE LIMITED TO ONLY A FRACTION OF THE MANY MARVELS THE UNIVERSE HAS TO SHOW YOU.

WHO KNOWS WHAT DESTINIES LIE ACROSS THIS INFINITE EXPANSE?

WHAT HIDES IN THE DARK?

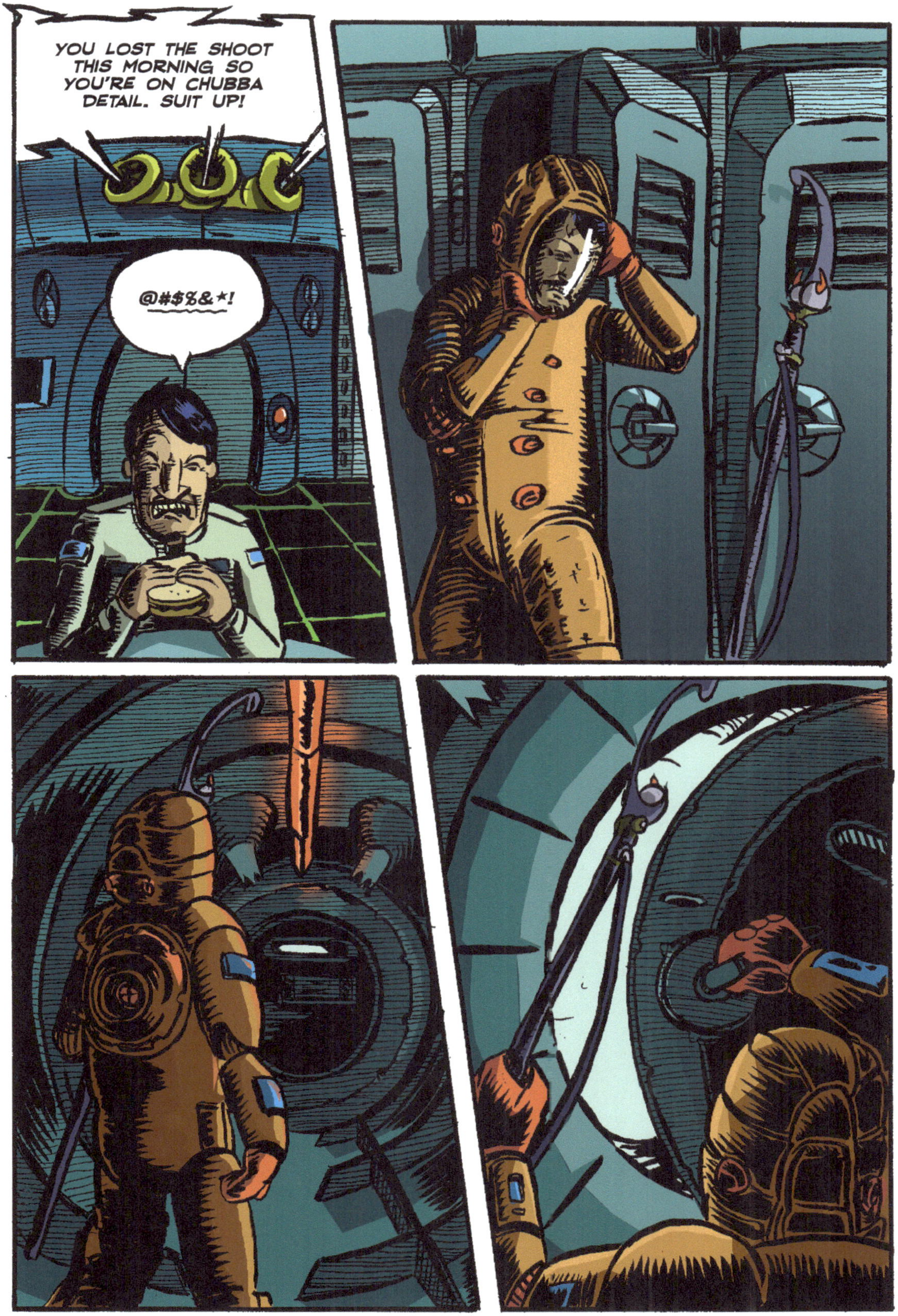
YOU LOST THE SHOOT THIS MORNING SO YOU'RE ON CHUBBA DETAIL. SUIT UP!
@#$%&*!

# SALVAGED HORIZON

Book One

STORY BY
BEN KUBCZAK

PICTURES BY
JAMES GREENE

MR LEON! CONTACT THE CONTROL NODE AND REQUEST PERMISSION TO DOCK.

AYE, SIR!

CREVEENA CONTROL, THIS IS HARVESTER SHIP *RATTOO* REQUESTING PERMISSION TO DOCK AT REFINERY BAY 7,

PERMISSION DENIED. ALL CIVILIAN TRAFFIC ORDERED TO HOLD POSITION. YOU WILL BE NOTIFIED WHEN WE GIVE THE ALL CLEAR.

HUH!

WELL, WHAT DO YOU THINK OF THAT, FELLAS?

SOUNDS LIKE SOME V.I.P. TRAFFIC IS COMIN' THRU.

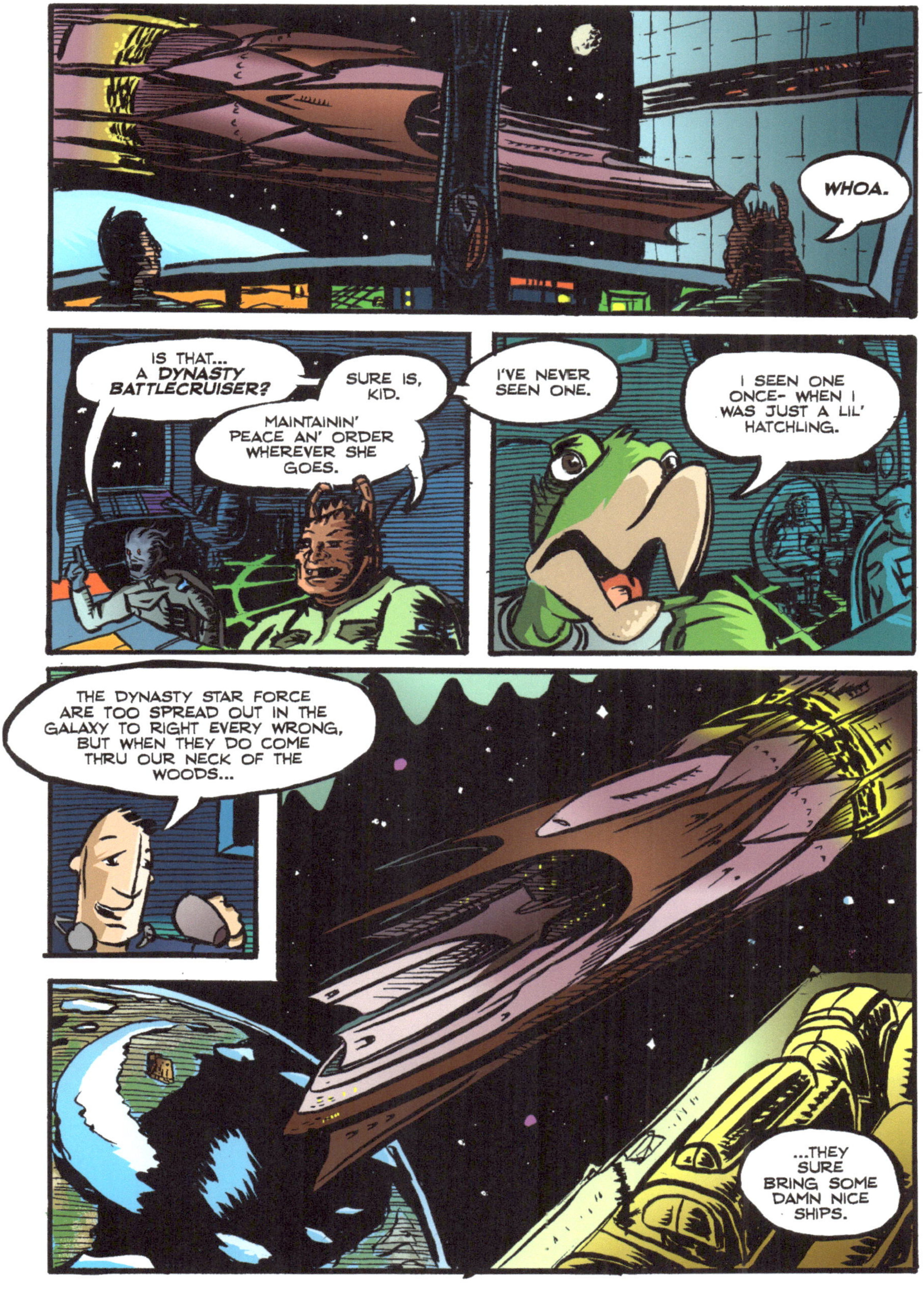

WHOA.

IS THAT... A *DYNASTY BATTLECRUISER?*

SURE IS, KID.

MAINTAININ' PEACE AN' ORDER WHEREVER SHE GOES.

I'VE NEVER SEEN ONE.

I SEEN ONE ONCE- WHEN I WAS JUST A LIL' HATCHLING.

THE DYNASTY STAR FORCE ARE TOO SPREAD OUT IN THE GALAXY TO RIGHT EVERY WRONG, BUT WHEN THEY DO COME THRU OUR NECK OF THE WOODS...

...THEY SURE BRING SOME DAMN NICE SHIPS.

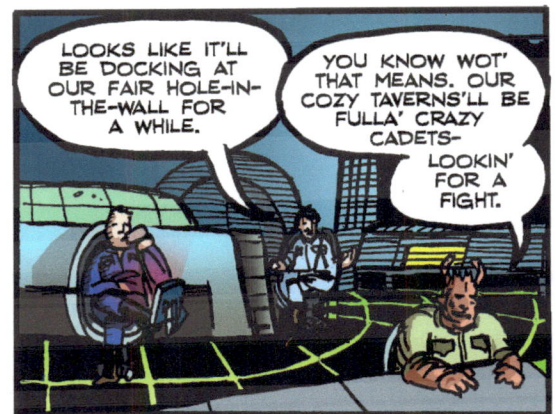

ANOTHER SUCCESSFUL VOYAGE, RETURNING FROM THE DEPTHS OF SPACE WITH A HOLD FULL OF RICHES.

ALLRIGHT, CREW. WE'LL SEE YOU BACK HERE TOMORROW MORNING AT 0800 HOURS FOR ANOTHER ONE.

MR. O'CHANG! YOU ARE ON SHIP-DUTY TONIGHT. SEE THAT THE CARGO TRANFER PROCEEDS SMOOTHLY.

AYE, SIR!

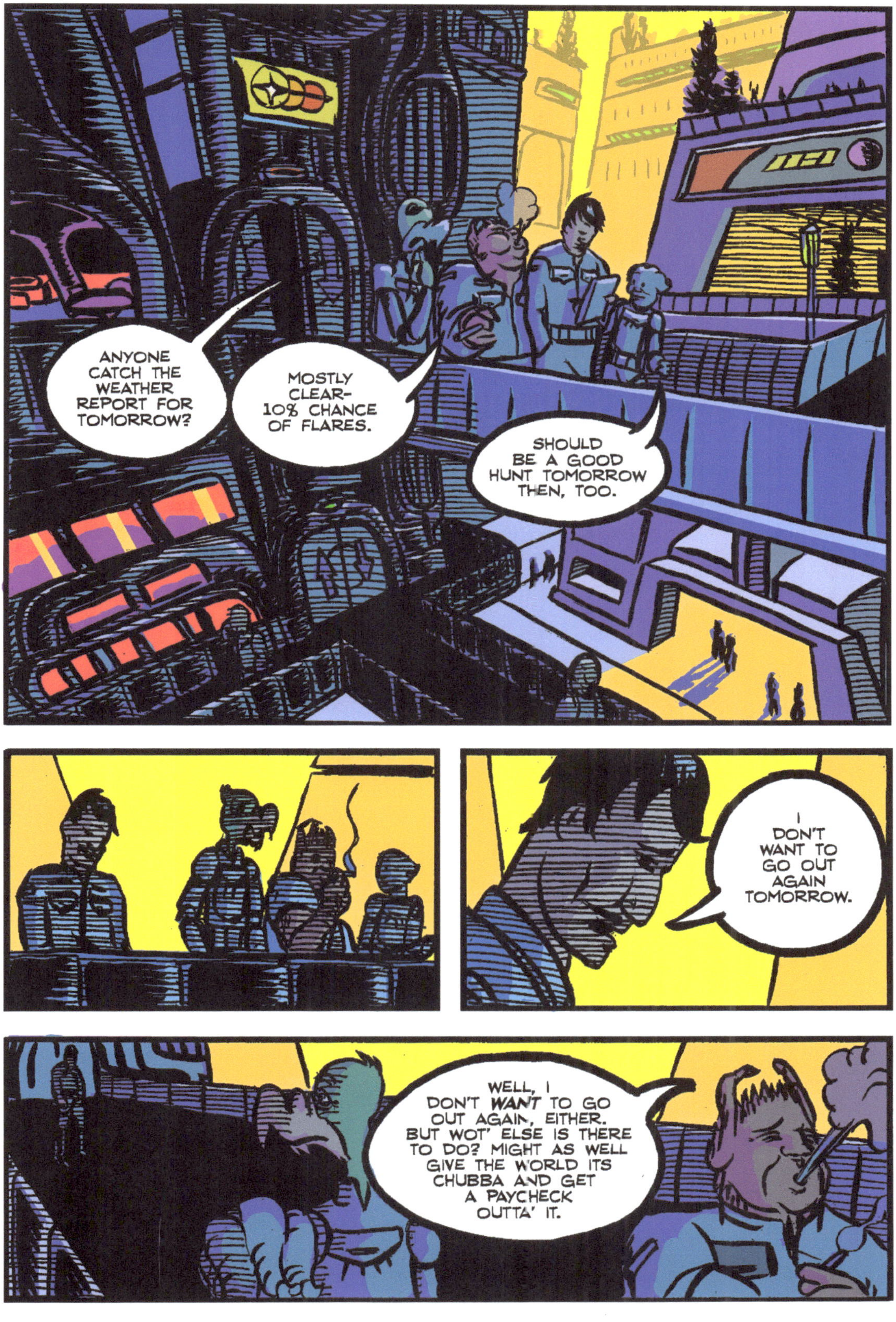

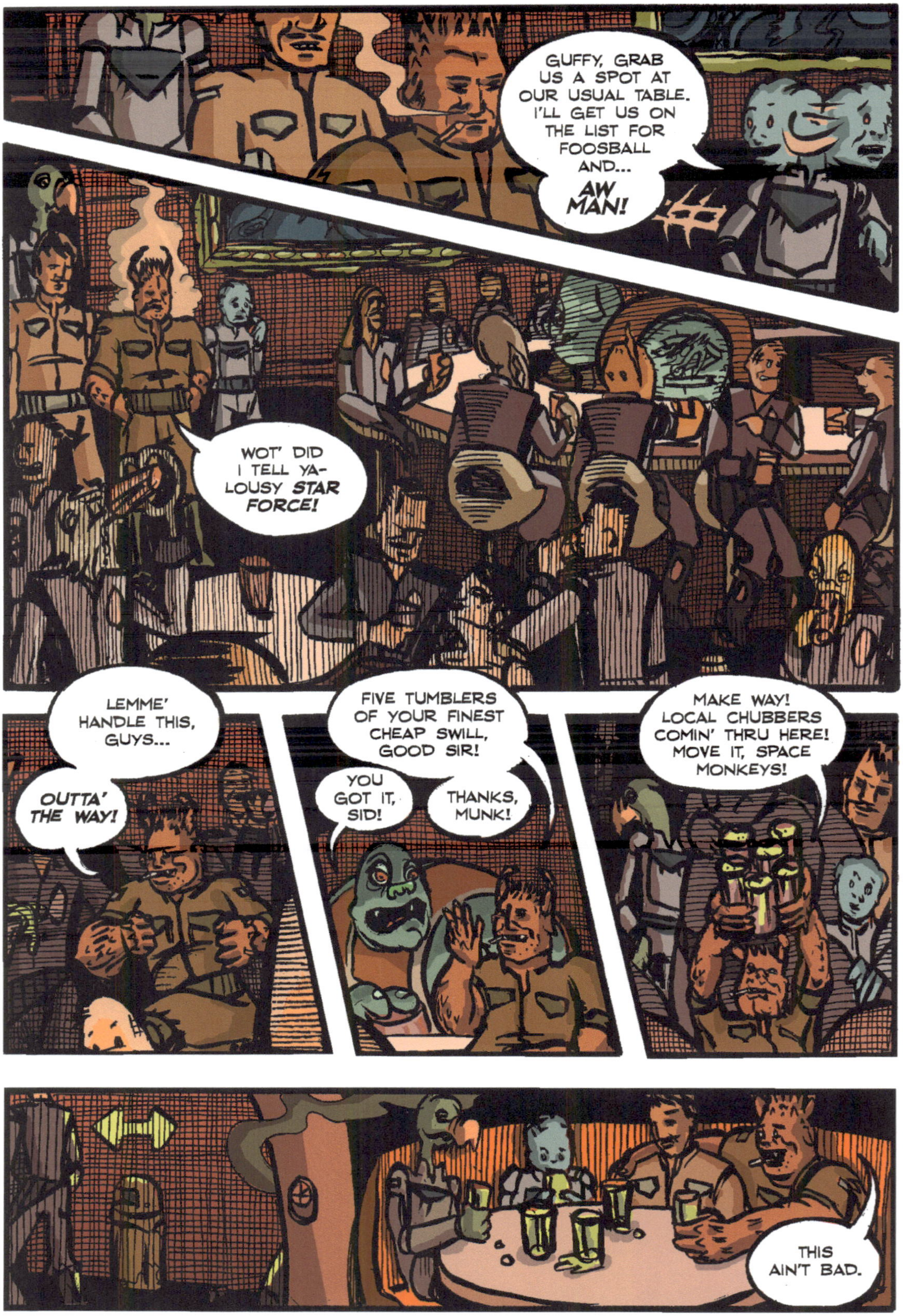

FROM WHAT I'VE LEARNED, THE ORIGINAL PONCE DE LEÓN WAS A FAMOUS EXPLORER- BUT NOT EVEN A SPACE EXPORER. I GUESS HE DIDN'T DO MUCH IN THE GRAND SCHEME OF UNIVERSAL HISTORY, BUT AT LEAST HE LED A TRULY ADVENTUROUS LIFE.

SEEMS PRETTY CRUEL TO CLONE AN EXPLORER IN A UNIVERSE THAT'S ALREADY BEEN EXPLORED.

AND WHY SUCH AN INSIGNIFICANT ONE, I WONDER?

WOT'D I TELL YA? *CLONE COMPLEX!*

BEINGS ARE ALWAYS MAKING CLONES OF EARLIER DEAD BEINGS THINKING THAT THEY CAN BRING 'EM BACK TO LIFE, BUT...

THEY SPEND THE REST OF THEIR LIVES FEELING LIKE THEY'RE NOT LIVING UP TO SOME SPECIAL *DESTINY.*

URP!

WELL, "CLONE COMPLEX" OR NOT, I'M GETTING SICK AND TIRED OF CHUBBA RUNS!

I HEAR YA- I WOULDN'T MIND A LITTLE ADVENTURE MYSELF.

HYUK! SAME HERE!

WHAT I'D GIVE FOR A LIFE WHERE THE HIGH-LIGHT OF MY DAY ISN'T BEING SUMMON-ED BY SPACEPORT SECURITY!

FWAP!

WELL, LET'S SEE HOW MUCH I OWE THIS TIME...

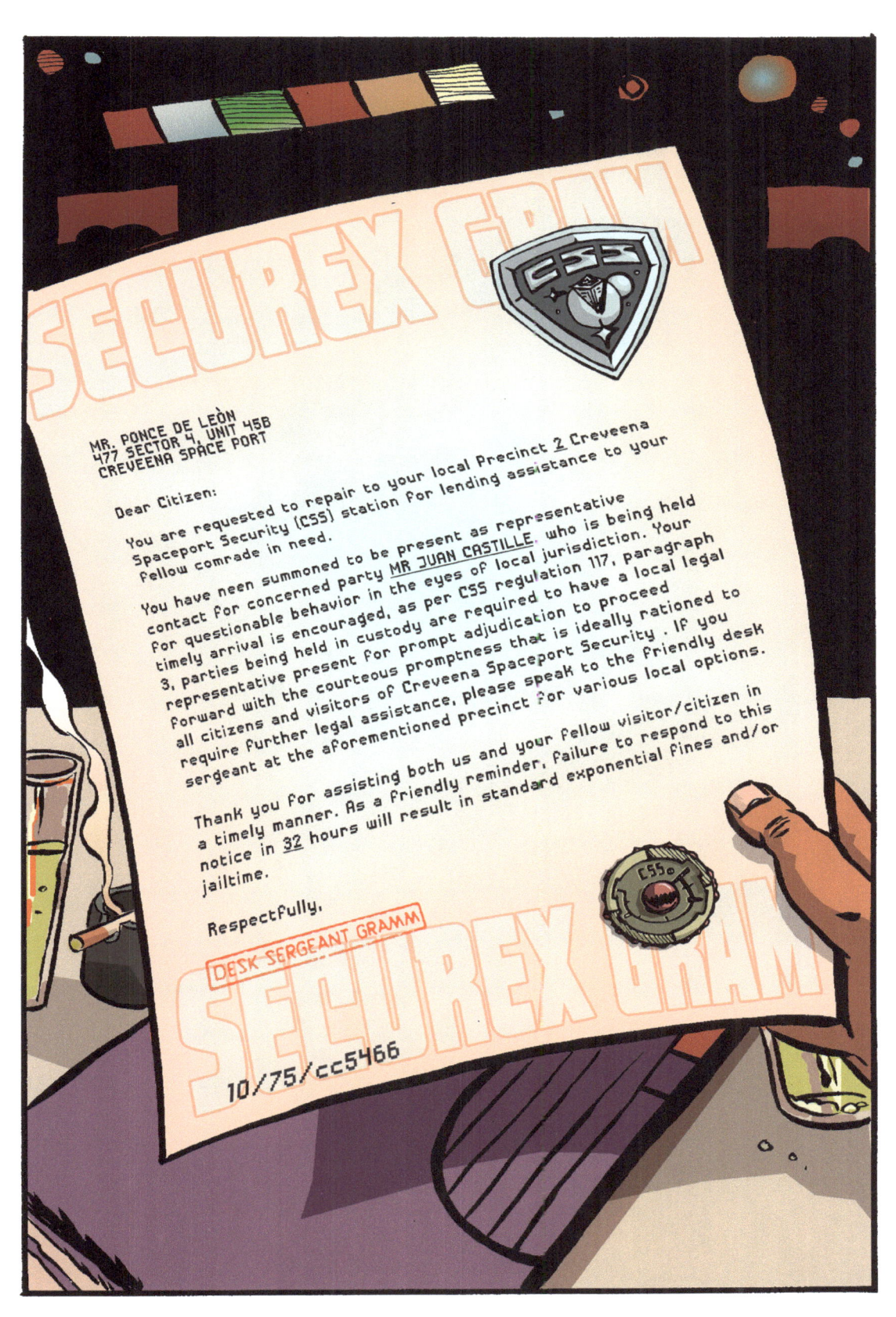

PRECINCT

SIGH...

ER, HI. I'M CITIZEN DE LEON PRESENTING MYSELF AS REQUESTED TO BE, UM, A REPRESENTATIVE CONTACT FOR ZAAFUR, ER, I MEAN *CASTILLE*...

HRRRM...

AH, WELL, YES. IT'S ABOUT TIME A CITIZEN REP SHOWED UP FOR HIM...

...HE'S IN CELL NUMBER 8 DOWN THIS HALLWAY. GET IN THERE AND SHUT HIM UP ALREADY! AFTER YOU'VE HAD A CHANCE TO COUNSEL, I CAN PROVIDE A LIST OF SOME QUALITY ASYLUMS DOWN ON HOMEGROUND CREVEENA!

WHAT *IS* THIS?

WE ARE NOT SURE. IT IS NOT CRIMINAL EVIDENCE AND DOESN'T FALL UNDER ANY CATEGORY OF ILLEGAL SUBSTANCE AS FAR AS WE CAN TELL. ANYWAYS, IT'S YOURS NOW.

MAY I SEE THE PRISONER AGAIN?

I'M AFRAID NOT...

...THIS PRISONER HAS REVOKED ALL RIGHTS FOR FURTHER CONTACT OR COUNSEL FROM THE OUTSIDE WORLD. GOOD DAY.

BEEEEE EEE-

SMAK!

ALL RIGHT, HAVE IT YOUR WAY. THERE ARE PLENTY OF OTHER SMELLY WATERING HOLES IN THIS DUMP OF A TOWN, RIGHT, BOYS? LET'S BLOW. WE'LL SEE YOU AGAIN *REEEAL* SOON.

DON'T LET THE DOOR HIT YOU ON THE WAY OUT!

LATER...

ANOTHER ROUND FOR THE LOCAL BOYS— *ON THE HOUSE!*

...AND I'VE NEVER SEEN SOMEONE SHRINK BACK SO QUICKLY! HAHA HA! ALL BARK AND *NO* BITE!

GOTTA' VISIT THE HEAD AGAIN. BE RIGHT BACK.

HUR, HUR!

AYE, AYE *MY CAPTAIN!*

URP.

EXIT

WHA?!

SLAM!

WHOA... WAIT A MINUTE!

SPOIL MY FUN, WILL YA'? NO MATTER, BUTCHERING LOCAL SCUM IS MY *SECOND* FAVORITE THING TO DO ON SHORE LEAVE!

NOT SO TOUGH WITH-OUT YOUR PET GORILLA, EH? HAHA HA! BUT DON'T WORRY. YOUR FRIENDS WILL BE JOINING YOU SOON ENOUGH!

FZAP!

ARRGH!

HELLO, VLACK!

TNK!

CHOOM!

YOU WITCH!!
I SHOULDA' KILLED
YOU WHEN I HAD THE
CHANCE!

CHOOM!

BUT NOW
THAT SHIP HAS
SAILED, VLACK,

WELL THIS JUST KEEPS GETTING BETTER AND BETTER.

EXCUSE ME, OFFICER— WHAT HAPPENED?

FORCES UNKNOWN BROKE INTO THE STATION, KILLED ALL PERSONEL AND PRISONERS, THEN APPARENTLY SET OFF INCENDIARY BOMBS.

EGAD!

OUR RESIDENTIAL QUARTERS WERE DESTROYED TONIGHT IN THE SAME WAY! DO YOU THINK THERE'S SOME SORT OF CONNECTION?

SOUNDS LIKELY... YOU INVOLVED IN SOME SORT OF INTERPLANETARY CRIME SYNDICATE?

NO!

OKAY, I BELIEVE YOU. MOVE ALONG NOW, PLEASE.

BAH! STATION SECURITY AIN'T EQUIPPED TO HANDLE SOMETHING LIKE THIS.

IT'S LIKE SOME SORTA' CONSPIRACY, MAN! WHY WOULD THEY DO THIS? WHAT DID WE DO?

...THEN THEY RANSACKED THE PLACE AND FOUND RECORDS SAYING IT WAS TURNED OVER TO MY POSSESSION...

MAYBE IT HAS SOMETHING TO DO WITH THIS? MAYBE SOMEONE ELSE IS LOOKING FOR IT. THEY CAME TO THE STATION, KILLED THE CRAZY GUY WHO GAVE IT TO ME...

THEN JUST GET *RID* OF THAT THING, MAN! THROW IT AWAY! GIVE IT TO SOMEONE ELSE! SHOOT IT INTO SPACE!

CASTILLE GAVE IT AWAY TO ME, BUT THAT DIDN'T STOP HIM FROM BEING *MURDERED!*

THIS LOOKS LIKE THE WORK OF PROS! WE GOTTA' GET OUT OF HERE!

LET'S GET BACK TO THE *RATTOO*, MAN. MAYBE WE CAN CONVINCE SPANNER TO TAKE OFF FOR AN EXTRA-EARLY HARVEST THIS MORNING. Y'KNOW- TO GET AWAY FROM THE STATION AN' THINK THIS THRU.

ALRIGHT. WHERE ELSE DO WE HAVE LEFT TO GO ANYWAY?

JUST WAIT A JIFFY! IF THEY KNEW WHERE WE ALL LIVED, MAYBE THEY'RE BACK AT THE SHIP *RIGHT NOW!*

*MAYBE THEY BLEW UP THE RATTOO ALREADY!*

KID'S GOT A POINT THERE.

WELL, LIKE I SAID, WHERE ELSE CAN WE GO?

NOW LOOK, LET'S ALL GO IN NICE AND QUIET-LIKE. WE'LL STICK TO THE SHADOWS AND SCOPE THINGS OUT BEFORE WE BOARD THE SHIP, OKAY?

OKAY, BUT I DON'T LIKE THE LOOKS A' THIS.

*SHHHHHHH!*

GUFFY, HAVE YOU NOTICED ANYTHING *SUSPICIOUS* HAPPENING ABOARD THE RATTOO TONIGHT?

NO, P.D.! IT'S BEEN QUIET, JUST LIKE EVERY OTHER NIGHT. I'M JUST RUNNING REGULAR OL' SHIP CHORES.

*WHAT'S WITH YOU GUYS?*

WHY WERE YOU AWAY FROM THE SHIP?

CAPTAIN SPANNER SENT ME TO THE STOREYARDS FOR SOME FRESH REPAIR PARTS FOR OUR MAINTENANCE BAY.

THAT'S ALL, NOTHING OUT OF THE ORDINARY. SERIOUSLY, WHAT'S GOING ON? ARE YOU ALL BUZZING *CRAZY*?!

WHAT DO YOU THINK, P.D.?

WELL, IT'S A GOOD SIGN THAT GUFFY IS STILL ALIVE...

*BWHAT?!*

THE SOONER WE CAN GET OFF-STATION TO REGROUP, THE SOONER WE CAN FIGURE THIS OUT. WE CAN'T HIDE HERE FOREVER.

I'M WITH SID. I SAY WE MAKE A RUN FOR IT.

ALRIGHT... *LET'S GO!*

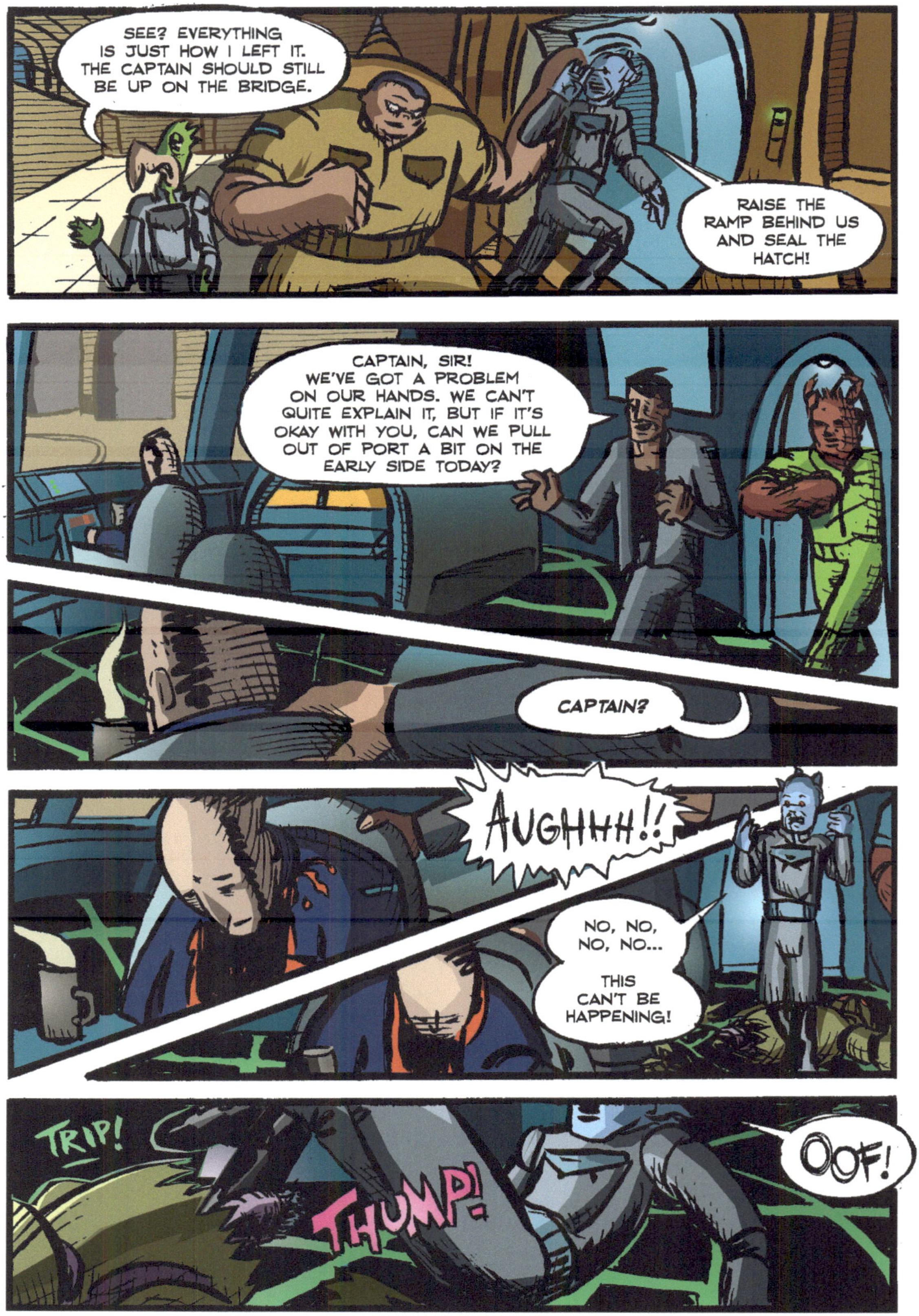

SEE? EVERYTHING IS JUST HOW I LEFT IT. THE CAPTAIN SHOULD STILL BE UP ON THE BRIDGE.

RAISE THE RAMP BEHIND US AND SEAL THE HATCH!

CAPTAIN, SIR! WE'VE GOT A PROBLEM ON OUR HANDS. WE CAN'T QUITE EXPLAIN IT, BUT IF IT'S OKAY WITH YOU, CAN WE PULL OUT OF PORT A BIT ON THE EARLY SIDE TODAY?

CAPTAIN?

AUGHHH!!

NO, NO, NO, NO...

THIS CAN'T BE HAPPENING!

TRIP!

THUMP!

OOF!

WHAT THE HECK IS *THAT*?! THAT WASN'T HERE BEFORE! AND THE CAPTAIN WASN'T DEAD BEFORE, EITHER!

IT'S A TOP-OF-THE-LINE ASSASSIN-BOT. ONLY THE RICHEST AND MOST POWERFUL PEOPLE HAVE ACCESS TO THESE. IT APPEARS THAT SOMEONE DOESN'T LIKE YOU.

HUBBA-BUBBA! AND WHO MIGHT YOU BE, MY LOVELY?

NAME'S *SURLY*...

WACK!

SORRY I DIDN'T SHOW UP SOON ENOUGH TO SAVE YOUR CAPTAIN. I DISCOVERED THE 'BOT JUST AFTER IT KILLED HIM. FORTUNATELY, I GOT THE DROP ON IT. GOOD THING, TOO. IT WOULD HAVE SELF-DESTRUCTED.

IT'S OKAY GUYS, WE'VE MET ALREADY.

I THINK SHE'S ON OUR SIDE.

I'M ON NOBODY'S SIDE BUT MINE. THIS ISN'T A SOCIAL CALL. YOU GOT IN THE WAY OF SOMEONE HUGE. NOW THEY'RE SENDING 'BOTS TO KILL ALL OF YOU.

NO ONE EVER SENDS JUST ONE, SO THIS STATION IS LIKELY CRAWLING WITH THEM. THERE MIGHT EVEN BE...

# ABOUT THE AUTHORS

BEN KUBCZAK IS AN ARCHITECT WHO CURRENTLY LIVES IN COLORADO WITH HIS LOVELY WIFE RACHEL AND THEIR TWO DEMANDING CATS. HE ENJOYS HIKING IN THE ROCKY MOUNTAINS AND DOESN'T MIND NOT BENG THE FIRST TO DO SO.

JAMES GREENE STUDIED FINE ART AT THE UNIVERSITY OF NORTHERN IOWA AND BECAME A CERTIFIED MASTER OF FINE ART AT THE UNIVERSITY OF TENNESSEE. HE CURRENTLY WORKS AS AN ARTIST AND EDUCATOR IN FLORIDA WHERE HE LIVES WITH HIS WIFE AND TWO SONS.

LIKE US ON FACEBOOK AT "MINDREADER COMICS"
AND EMAIL US WITH YOUR FEEDBACK AT
MINDREADERCOMICBOOKS@GMAIL.COM

www.ingramcontent.com/pod-product-compliance
Lightning Source LLC
Chambersburg PA
CBHW041538240626
47164CB00002B/54